To those who see Queens
- *LC*

To those who climbed mountains, slept under the stars and shared picnics with me,
and to the one who handed me endless jars of mint sauce with a spoon,
without judgement
- *NT*

First published in the United Kingdom in 2021 by Lantana Publishing Ltd.
www.lantanapublishing.com | info@lantanapublishing.com

American edition published in 2021 by Lantana Publishing Ltd., UK.

Distributed in the United States and Canada by Lerner Publishing Group, Inc.
241 First Avenue North, Minneapolis, MN 55401 U.S.A.
For reading levels and more information, look for this title at www.lernerbooks.com
Cataloging-in-Publication Data Available.

Hardback ISBN: 978-1-911373-88-9
eBook PDF: 978-1-911373-68-1
ePub3: 978-1-913747-53-4

Printed and bound in China
Original artwork created using mixed media, completed digitally

THE QUEEN ON OUR CORNER

Lucy Christopher & Nia Tudor

 Lantana

I've been trying to tell Ma about the Queen on our corner.

She's right there at the end of our road, in that plot of land that never got built on. She's sitting with her royal hound.

I didn't notice her before either.
Like everyone else, I just walked by.

Ma was scared of her at first. But the Queen on our corner
is just tired from all the battles she has fought and won,

and the ones she has fought and lost too.

Maybe she journeyed up all the great

rivers of the world to arrive exactly here.

I think the Queen on our corner
even fought dragons, swaying
and slaying on mountaintops,
while the rest of the world slept.

She journeyed all over, to all the hidden spots in the countries far away.

Our Queen has had more adventures than anyone!

But nobody around here knows this. Perhaps they can't see that she really is a queen at all. Like Ma couldn't once, either.

People around here say the
Queen should leave.

But our Queen doesn't
know where her palace
is anymore.

It's easy to lose a palace, that's what I say to Ma.
Easier than you might think.

So Ma and me stop and give her gifts, like you do with queens. Tea and toast for our wise woman of worlds. Crumbs for the royal hound.

She smiles and it's brilliant (even though she has lost some teeth in battle).

Sometimes she tells us stories about other corners,

ones that are shiny and
golden and full of light;

ones in the deepest,
darkest forests;

and ones in cities that
hum with noise.

At night, the Queen on our corner and her royal hound protect our street, keeping watch for danger. I know, because I've seen them.

And danger does come, one hot, dry night. When the wind is high, flames start from a forgotten match.

The fire spreads to the shop and edges closer.

The Queen and her
royal hound shout and
howl to wake all of us up.

Soon everyone is outside,
standing and shouting,
carrying buckets and hoses.

People are grabbing their precious things and taking their cats.
Then the fire trucks come.

They douse the flames, and say
it could have been worse.

People agree and shake
their heads and turn
for their houses.

But now it's my turn to shout!

I tell the people that our Queen saw the fire coming and warned us just in time.

She saved our homes.

The people on the street stop and look.
And then, they see her.

They thank the Queen finally.

They give her water and blankets, but I know
that what she wants best is her own palace.

So we build her one. Right there on the corner.

Nobody walks by anymore.

Instead, we thank the Queen on our corner
and listen to her stories.

These days, the Queen makes tea for Ma and me
and even the royal hound.

Ma and the Queen keep watch over the whole street
and laugh together like parrots, while the royal hound
and me eat the leftovers.

(Though she still fights the odd battle!)

Dear Reader,

My inspiration for this story came from several places: a friend's story about a soldier living rough; a hairdresser who spent weekends voluntarily cutting hair for the homeless; and a musician who wanted to play me his saxophone but who'd had to sell it to survive.

Soon, I started to notice the 'kings and queens' all around my town, tucked into doorways or perched in corners of carparks. They got me thinking – who might these people be if they had a bed, a haircut, a saxophone? Could I help them find out? The answer to this question is a life's work but, as often as I can, I try to be like the child in my story. I look for the value in everyone who shares our streets. I look for the Queens.

You can look too!

Lucy